MINI SAGAS

THE ADVENTURE STARTS HERE ...

TALES FROM CHESHIRE

First published in Great Britain in 2009 by
Young Writers, Remus House, Coltsfoot Drive,
Peterborough, PE2 9JX
Tel (01733) 890066 Fax (01733) 313524
All Rights Reserved

FOREWORD

Since Young Writers was established in 1990, our aim has been to promote and encourage written creativity amongst children and young adults. By giving aspiring young authors the chance to be published, Young Writers effectively nurtures the creative talents of the next generation, allowing their confidence and writing ability to grow.

With our latest fun competition, *The Adventure Starts Here...*, primary school children nationwide were given the tricky challenge of writing a story with a beginning, middle and an end in just fifty words.

The diverse and imaginative range of entries made the selection process a difficult but enjoyable task with stories chosen on the basis of style, expression, flair and technical skill. A fascinating glimpse into the imaginations of the future, we hope you will agree that this entertaining collection is one that will amuse and inspire the whole family.

CONTENTS

The Meadows Primary School

THE MINI SAGAS

HUMPFREY DUMPFREY

Scorching hot morning and Humpfrey Dumpfrey was boiling over, so he flung himself on the wall. Suddenly the football whacked him on the head, shattering Humphrey into tiny pieces. Quickly the football team ran to see what had happened. An impossible task to piece him together, leaving him to die.

KAYLEIGH ILLINGWORTH (11)

Brookside Primary School

A YELLOW GLOW!

I was sitting on a bench, in the park, next to a rusty
bin. For a second I saw a yellow glow and a gust of
wind blew me into the glow! I was in a tornado.
'Help!' I gasped. Nobody came. A door hit me in the
head and …

SAMUEL BERNDT (10)
Brookside Primary School

MAGICAL WATER WORLD

Swaying palm trees were standing under the blazing red sunlight. Slowly and steadily the tide was breaking free from the deep blue ocean. Gracefully the dolphins leaped into the fresh air. Splashing, almost silently, they dived into the water world. Filling this magical place; starfish, coral and much more.

JESSICA BRADBURY (11)

Brookside Primary School

GHOST

Lying in my bed, I saw a ghost! Silently it floated around my room, not seeming to notice me. I looked around making sure it did not see me. Making as little noise as I could, I crept to the door. Effortlessly it sensed me and turned. It grabbed me ...

ELLA DIANE CREWS (10)
Brookside Primary School

HORROR STRIKES

Slowly I woke up. Creeping downstairs, I heard a loud thud from my room, it was … ? It looked like a coffin and a key, I tried it, it fitted the lock. I opened it, a creature with talons as toes and fingers. I sat up then slowly passed out!

PETER WHITEHEAD (10)

Brookside Primary School

THE THREE LITTLE PIGS WITH A TWIST

Holidaying for fun, the three pigs set off. Hiding next door the devious wolf was waiting for food with coal for fur and fierce fire eyes. Pouncing on the unsuspecting pigs, blood shot everywhere. Gasping for air they got caught! Surprisingly not one survived. Turning to bacon, he ate them.

MEGAN PENNINGTON (10)

Brookside Primary School

CREATURE

I slowly opened my eyes. There in front of me was
the strangest creature I'd ever seen. There it was,
swimming in the clear water, its shimmery tail shining
like a star. I reached out and touched it. Suddenly it
took me with it to the land of my dreams.

NATASHA PRINCE (10)

Brookside Primary School

A MONSTER

One minute I was paddling in the sea, suddenly
a monster appeared on the beach. I screamed. I
was the only one left, left on the beach, deserted. I
screamed for help. The monster chased me around
the beach. I screamed but no one returned.

AMBER SEDDON (10)
Brookside Primary School

A HOUSE IN THE CORNER

Nobody knows what's in that house but I'm determined to find out. Creeping silently along the cliff edge my stomach turns to lead with fear. Opening by itself, the door creaks. Walking in, will I regret this? Suddenly something swoops past me. Jumping back in horror my heart stops beating ...

JOANNE FULTON (11)
Brookside Primary School

9

THE BIKE RIDE

Quickly I was riding down a hill to a farm and my sister lost her helmet. I was going full speed and I fell over her helmet. I flipped over my bike frame. My leg was dripping with blood but I will always love bike riding.

ZAHRA LONGDON (8)

Brookside Primary School

THE BIG SWIM

The aircraft started to judder like a bomb exploding.
Next minute we were plunging down like a lightning
bolt! We landed in the sea and had to swim six
hundred meters to the land.

ALEXANDER BARKE (7)
Brookside Primary School

HALLOWE'EN

The spooky castle is covered in dirty clouds, it is very scary. The whistling wind is blowing the leaves off the trees into the pond. Bats are flapping around my head as I walk nervously up the path. I knock and the door creaks open.
'Trick or treat!' I smiled.

HANNAH BOARDMAN (8)
Brookside Primary School

TILLY CAT GETS STUCK

Tilly went on a walk to the park but on her way she saw four unpleasant guests, they were dogs! Tilly was really scared so she started to miaow.
Six minutes later a man came and scared the dogs away. The man took Tilly home. She never went alone again.

LUCIE BERNDT (8)
Brookside Primary School

RUNNING AWAY FROM HOME

I was running away from home. I couldn't see anything, it was pitch-black. I ran up to the darkest castle in history. I eventually got to the castle; a shiver went down my back.
'Ha! Ha! Ha!'
I ran back as fast as I could.

ISOBEL SHERRATT-COUSINS (8)
Brookside Primary School

LABORATORY EXPLOSION

Slowly, a scientist came into the lab. He felt damp.
There was a massive explosion. The scientist flew
out of the building and broke his arm and leg.
At the hospital he was in pain.
In a month he was safe and sound. He looked like a
horse, but lived.

DANIEL SHERRATT-COUSINS (7)
Brookside Primary School

THE CAR ACCIDENT

I was walking across the golden gate bridge. Suddenly Sam shouted, 'The car is out of control!' I told my family to run but it was too late, the car hit me! I went flying into the river.

Jo said, 'Alex, call the lifeboats to come save him.'

NATHAN EDWARDS (9)

Brookside Primary School

THE BIKE RIDE

Nathan and Ryan went on a bike ride to High Lane
Park to go on the ramps. Ryan shouted to Nathan,
'I'm going up the biggest ramp of them all.'
A minute later, 'Argh!' Ryan had fallen off the ramp
and broke his arm.
Five minutes later the ambulance arrived.

RYAN CREWS (8)
Brookside Primary School

THE BIG MATCH

What a hit! The big red corky went flying through the air. Charlie made a six. He only needed two more sixes to win the game but on the fourth run Charlie slipped and fell over. The first-aider man came, Charlie had broken his arm!

CHARLIE PODOLANSKI (9)

Brookside Primary School

IT'S SNOWING!

Crystal snowflakes fell to the ground.
'Look Mum, it's snowing. Can I go out please?'
'Yes, but get your hat on.'
I'm ready.
'First I will make a snow angel called Millie. Then I'll
make a snowman with green and blue buttons. I'll call
him Bob.'

ISABELLA STANYER (9)

Brookside Primary School

THE SMASHED STAR

It was a week before Christmas and I was decorating the Christmas tree with baubles, tinsel and lights. When I went to put the star on the top I couldn't reach so I stood on the sofa.

'Ouch!' I felt the star slip and smash on the floor!

YASMIN CRAWFORD (7)
Brookside Primary School

HUMPTY DUMPTY

One day Humpty Dumpty saw a speck coming his way, speeding fast. It knocked him right off the wall. Just then the realised the speck was a spaceship with an alien in it. The alien tried to put him together but he couldn't!

TOM SHEPHERDSON (7)

Brookside Primary School

LISA'S HAUNTED HORROR

Lisa walked silently into the abandoned house; she walked up the rusty stairs then she realised it was her house!
Suddenly something or someone screamed, Lisa ran up the stairs, there, spinning slowly was a body hanging! Lisa saw a dagger in her back, she screamed then blacked out.

CHLOE BRIDGE (11)
Great Moor Junior School

THE DAY OF THE NINJA GRANNY DREAM

Jack and Sam were on holiday together and came across an old retirement home. It was battered and destroyed 'Let's go in,' said Jack and Sam. Quietly they opened the door. Suddenly, a whole army of ninja grannies sprung out and destroyed the Earth. Of course, it was a dream!

JACK BANCROFT (10)

Great Moor Junior School

LOVE IN POTS

I woke up, my mum was gleaming.
'We're there Jess.'
Mum picked up her bag and jumped off the plane. I
gloomily followed.
My mum and dad split two years ago when I was
twelve. I don't know where he is but I know where
me and mum are!

CHLOË BROWN (11)

Great Moor Junior School

THE HAUNTED HOUSE

David and Carly opened the door, the door creaked.
David slowly tiptoed in with Carly following not far
behind. Carly insisted that they should go, David
carried on like he was deaf.
Suddenly a ghost jumped out at them. 'Argh!' they
went. Josh lifted his cloak up, they both ran.

SAUL ASHTON (11)
Great Moor Junior School

ABANDONED FUN

'Hello? Is anyone there?' James was in an abandoned
warehouse, in the middle of nowhere.
'Go away,' said a voice.
'OK, umm … sorry.'
Donk! The door was bolted shut. The lights switched
off and on.
'Decided to stay? Game on!'
'OK,' murmured James. He lost.
'Argh!'
'James, time for school.'

HARRY FLYNN (10)
Great Moor Junior School

ARNOLD'S TRIP

Arnold was the eldest of three brothers. Sam, Grant
and him.
One day, they went to America and met Mickey
Mouse. They got his autograph.
When they go back to their hotel, they heard there
was going to be a tornado.
However, they got lucky and arrived in England
safely.

SCOTT MCCORMACK (10)

Great Moor Junior School

LITTLE RED AND THE BEANSTALK

The wolf stared at Little Red Riding Hood, carefully scanning the basket she held.

'Go away,' she yelled and threw her shoe at him hard, aiming at his nose. She ran, a cookie fell on the floor and there before her lay a huge beanstalk. She fell, the wolf pounced!

ABBEY JENKINS (11)

Great Moor Junior School

WAR IN THE WOODS

Boom! went the grenade as one of the soldiers threw
it at the enemy. I lay there under the plants and the
dark leafless trees, gun in hand, waiting for it to
end. I crawled through the undergrowth to a tree.
Suddenly the siren went, the game had finished!

SAM RIDGWAY (11)
Great Moor Junior School

THE FORBIDDEN MONSTER

I was excited; my friend was here for a sleepover.
We were chatting when suddenly we heard a whistle
from behind the door. Then a flash of green light
filled the room. A monster came in.
'Hello boys,' it said. It was only Dad back from the
spooky disco.

SIRAAJ IDREES (9)

Mersey Vale Primary School

THE JEWEL SISTERS

Sapphire and Crystal were best friends.
'Sapphire we always have a sleepover at your
mansion in the holidays. This year we could camp in
my garden,' Crystal said.
'We'll do it tonight,' Sapphire exclaimed.
Later, Sapphire arrived early and hid in the tent. As
Crystal arrived, Sapphire screamed …

EMMILY FOWLER (10)

Mersey Vale Primary School

THE SPOOKY HALLOWE'EN

One dark night two girls went trick or treating. The first door they went to didn't open. They knocked on the door again, nobody answered so they went to another house. Nobody replied. They headed back when somebody tapped them on the shoulder. They looked back …

LAYAN AL-MUSA ALKAHATANI

Mersey Vale Primary School

THE SPELL THAT WENT WRONG

In her house making a spell, all of a sudden Winnie heard a *bang!* She was a bit shocked but she carried on anyway.

Later she put the potion on her favourite plant. The following morning she went outside and looked at the plant. Nothing had happened ... 'Argh! It's alive!'

LAURYN PETTIFER (9)

Mersey Vale Primary School

JIMMY THE HAMSTER AND HIS NEW DRESS

One day Jimmy, Tom's hamster, woke up, feeling peculiar. He thought he was wearing a dress! Although Tom had gone to school, could he be playing a trick on him? Suddenly Tom's mum came in and took a picture of Jimmy. Jimmy realised he was wearing a dress! But why?

ZARAH ISLAM (10)

Mersey Vale Primary School

SPACE 1

One day, high above the Earth, a man and his team, Ishraq, John and Siraaj were stranded. They were trying to get back to Earth. No matter what they tried nothing seemed to work. Suddenly *crash!*
'Waah! Whoa!' screamed John.
'What's g-g-going on?' screamed Ishraq and then …

ISHRAQ CHOUDHURY (8)

Mersey Vale Primary School

WILLIAM AND THE ALIENS

William was fourteen and lived in Manhattan. One day he was abducted from school by aliens who took him to Planet Zonk. They imprisoned him in a marshmallow jail. William hungrily bit the wall. He made a hole and ran to the time portal which teleported him back to Manhattan.

MATTHEW MUIRHEAD (10)

Moorfield Primary School

SUSHI PEOPLE

One day I woke up in a completely different world from my own. The mini sushi people called it Sushi Land because everything was made out of sushi. Ten minutes later I turned into sushi myself. I was tempted to eat myself but I knew not to. I lived happily.

ANNA SYLVESTER (11)
Moorfield Primary School

THE HOMESICK CAT

There was a cat called Beth. She decided to run away. She ran away to a faraway place and didn't come back for a long time. She made a big mistake. She went back home to see her mum and dad. She was very, very, very happy again.

ABI JOYNSON (10)
Moorfield Primary School

THE RAT

Once there lived a rat called Mortimer, he was tired of having his home (the bins) destroyed. He made a plan.
One day Mortimer climbed into the dustbin truck and turned off the machine.
He did this every day until the dustbin men stopped coming to his street.

KARL HURSTFIELD (10)
Moorfield Primary School

HUMPTY DUMPTY

One day Humpty Dumpty went out to play in the sunny weather. He sat on a wall and suddenly slipped and cracked. All of the king's horses and men came rushing to help him but they couldn't put him back together again. They went home miserable.

UJJAL HUSSAIN (11)
Moorfield Primary School

THE MONKEY WITH NO TAIL

There's a monkey who has no tail, he gets picked on by the other monkeys. Everytime he tries to swing on the branches he falls.
One day he saw a figure shaped like a banana. It said some words and *poof!* He had a tail. He was so amazed.

ALEX ROBERTS (10)
Moorfield Primary School

THE HAUNTED MANSION IN ASIA

There was a mansion in the woods. One night three boys went in; they were in the door, it shut! The boys froze in terror. A howl came from upstairs. The boys were scared. One tripped on a hammer then smashed the window and they all ran.

MATTHEW BUTTON (10)

Moorfield Primary School

AN ANIMAL STORY

This is a story about a monkey, a lion and a snake. They get hit by lightning, on a stormy night in the jungle, and develop super powers. From that day on there was never any chaos in the jungle. If there was then it would be stopped right away!

JACOB BAZELL (10)

Moorfield Primary School

SCAMP THE SUPERDOG

On a little street called Cloverbank, there lived a
three-legged dog named Scamp. No dogs liked him.
He couldn't run as fast as the others.
One day Doris, the fairy dogmother, waved her
magic bone. Scamp could fly! From then on he was
known as Scamp the Superdog.

NICK BARRATT (11)

Moorfield Primary School

THE COFFIN

One night Tom was walking home from the park. A noise! He stopped, turned and ran from the horrific sight of a coffin floating towards him. He ran home and up into the bathroom. He grabbed the cough medicine, threw it ... the coffin stopped, stopped floating. He was relieved.

JORDAN LAVERTY (10)
Moorfield Primary School

THE MASSAGE

There was a lady that was going for a massage.
The man doing the massage did it so relaxing it put
the lady to sleep. He intended to do that and he
kidnapped her.
There was a huge search for her. The police finally
found her and arrested the man.

MURRAY TUPMAN (11)

Moorfield Primary School

GHOSTLY GOINGS ON

My dad lived in an old farmhouse with his two brothers and his parents. One night, whilst everyone was sleeping, he was lying in his bed. He must have been dreaming because he saw an old figure go through the wall of his mum's bedroom! Now that is spooky stuff.

BRANDON BARRINGTON-WOOD (10)
Moorfield Primary School

THE MASTER

Boom! The Lardis landed by a mysterious spacecraft, in the atomic air. Wocter Dho strolled out and there in front of him was a Gailic and a Fyberman. The Wocter used his toffee screwdriver and turned them into gummy bears. He gobbled them and became Ultimate Master *again!*

JAC SCOTT (10)
Navigation Primary School

THE CURSE

In the deserted desert, two explorers ran to the spot
and started digging. They dug till their arms ached.
Suddenly they hit a box.
'Ouch!' the box shouted.
The two explorers hurled out the box but an eagle
swooped down and speared the box. A powder
came out, a curse!

EMMA DRAINEY (9)
Navigation Primary School

THE THINGS IN MY WARDROBE

I awoke to a rattling sound from my wardrobe. I slowly approached it. *Dare I open the doors?* I thought. I finally plucked up the courage and opened the doors. Suddenly all sorts of terrifying creatures jumped out, paranormals and apparitions. They took me into a parallel universe …

RORY MACKENZIE (9)

Navigation Primary School

THE CREAKING DOOR

I was shaking nervously on the cream couch while
the door kept creaking loudly!
I grabbed my soft teddy bear as quickly as I could
and slowly tiptoed to the door. I shakily put my hand
onto the door handle. The house was dead quiet.
Suddenly the door swung open ...

MEGAN DEE (10)
Navigation Primary School

MY LAST DAY

It was a boiling day; the sun was blazing down on me. I was paragliding in the air. I was gliding cheerfully when suddenly the parachute ripped! Slowly and silently I rapidly fell to my death!

MAISIE MCNAB (9)
Navigation Primary School

THE MYSTERIOUS HOUSE

One blazing hot sunny day I was feeling spooked because the curtains closed by themselves. I was with my friend and he was scared too. I went upstairs and everything was gone, everything had become dust. Suddenly I cried down the squeaky stairs to tell my friend, he had disappeared!

SHIVRAJ MAHINDA (9)

Navigation Primary School

THE DESTROYING DUO

Bang! A huge terrifying monster came crashing through the volcano's side! It was knocking trees down on its way towards Cameron and Joe. With their powerful double-barrelled gun they shot the monster, but more monsters came smashing trees towards them. Suddenly all the monsters dropped to the ground!

JOSEPH HILTON (9)

Navigation Primary School

THE HOUSE OF DEATH

Today I was walking down the road peacefully. The sun was shining down on me but when I turned to my right I saw a dark gloomy house with smashed windows and chipped paint. The roof was battered but I took the risk and slowly walked inside the horrible house …

LAUREN HUTCHINSON (9)
Navigation Primary School

AROUND THE WORLD IN A DAY

There was a tiny boy called Tom and he wanted to go
around the world in a day.
'Well, it will take me eight hours to get to America,
three hours to get to Scotland ... '
Tom's mum caught him talking to himself.
Unfortunately, Tom couldn't travel around the world!

JAMES ABBEY (9)

Navigation Primary School

THE BABYSITTER

The old grumpy man came to babysit; slowly he
put the baby back in the cot and walked over to the
window. He saw a man holding a knife and a baby.
The man was about to kill the baby when he realised
he was staring into an old mirror ...

OLIVIA MCLEAN (9)
Navigation Primary School

THE GRAVEYARD

'Argh! A snake, no a leech!'
'Run rapidly,' shouted Rob.
They ran into a zombie. They left screaming,
scattering rocks to remember their tracks therefore
the dumb zombies followed the rocks.
Were the children home? No! They were in a box!
Clumsily the zombies walked towards them …

THOMAS BAXTER (8)

Navigation Primary School

MR LONGWORTH

Mr Longworth looked at me menacingly. I felt scared.
He walked carefully over to me trying not to smirk.
In a deep terrifying voice, he bellowed,
'Have you learnt your hard spellings?'
'Yes, I've learnt them.'
I struggled with them immensely. He wasn't very
pleased with my spelling at all!

MEGAN WARMISHAM (9)
Navigation Primary School

THE MISSING PUPPY

Rosie, the puppy belonged to Livvy. Rosie went off
for a long walk after being told off by Livvy's mum.
Rosie was cross with Livvy because she had blamed
the mess on her. Rosie decided to run away.
The next morning, Livvy shouted, 'Where's my
puppy? I want my puppy!'

CHLOE HIGGINS (8)
Navigation Primary School

BACK TO THE TITANIC

I opened my eyes, feeling seasick. I was on a boat, at the bottom of the sea! How? To my surprise I could breathe. I spun around to come up against skeletons. Swimming away from the ship I saw the name - Titanic! Shocked, scared, alone, a long lonely death ...

SHANNON CHRISCOLI (10)
Our Lady's Catholic Primary School

THE HAUNTED MUSEUM

I stepped forward, the mummy's tomb staring at me. I ran, the hairs on my legs were standing up tall. I walked slowly to the blinding black room where the mummy lay. Entering the room I tiptoed up to the mummy's tomb. It was open but where was the mummy?

BETHANY FAIRCLOUGH (10)

Our Lady's Catholic Primary School

SUPER CAT TO THE RESCUE

Super Cat flew towards the Eiffel Tower where a hot
air balloon had landed. The driver couldn't get down.
Super Cat flew up and grabbed the driver and placed
her on the ground.
'Thanks Super Cat,' everyone shouted.
'No problem,' said Super Cat and shot off home
towards the sun.

MADELINE WILLIAMSON-GERRARD (10)
Our Lady's Catholic Primary School

EVIL LAUGH

Suddenly the door shut behind me. I heard an evil laugh. It came closer and closer. A hand tapped me on the back. I turned around - nothing there. I heard another evil laugh. I ran upstairs. It followed me. I started to scream. I stopped, the laughing stopped ...

SAFFRON HIBBERT (10)
Our Lady's Catholic Primary School

THE GHOST

It was an ordinary day in America when people suddenly started to believe there was a ghost. I didn't believe them at first until strange things started to happen in my bedroom. Things moved on their own! Was the nightmare coming back? Has it come to get me?

SOPHIE DAVIES (10)
Our Lady's Catholic Primary School

THE SCORPION

The sun mercilessly feasted upon my head. Although
I was tired I pressed on, only to find a boy in front
of me covered in blood. My face went red as fire. I
slowly turned around. A shiver ran down my spine.
There it was, the scorpion. I screamed!

TOMMY RYAN (10)
Our Lady's Catholic Primary School

LOST

Once, when the world was young, there was a young
girl called Paige. She got hopelessly lost in a forest
and couldn't find her way out. Suddenly she heard
rustling in the bushes and out came a girl. She said,
'Hello, my name is Zoe.'
'Hello, my name is Paige.'

SHELLEY BROCKLEHURST (10)
Our Lady's Catholic Primary School

THE DEAD

There was a man who died at one hundred and came alive at night. He killed men!
One day the police caught him and put him in prison but he escaped and left a note saying he'd gone to his grave. He never came back ever again.

TOM SHIPPAM (8)

St Catherine of Siena RC Primary School, Lowton

POOR RUDOLPH

Once there was a reindeer called Rudolph and he
had seven other brothers.
One day Rudolph was lying down when two of his
brothers came along.
'Rudolph, move your butt,' said one of them.
'I want to lie down,' said the other.
Poor Rudolph started to cry and ran away.

FINLAY STEWART (8)
St Catherine of Siena RC Primary School, Lowton

MR MAGIC

Mr Magic was trying a new spell on his best friend.
The spell went 'Hocus pocus, dibbly doo, here's a
spell just for you. Oh no, he's a frog!'
A witch told him to say it backwards.
'OK, you for just spell a here's, doo dibbly, pocus,
hocus. That's better!'

PAUL GREAVES (9)
St Peter's Catholic Primary School, Stalybridge

70

FRANKENZILLA

There was a scientist called Dr Jove. He used the
phone and ordered a spicy pepperoni pizza.
Three minutes later the pizza arrived and Dr Jove
took the pizza. He fell backwards into a pot of acid
and turned into a hideous monster.

DANIEL JOHNSTON (9)

St Peter's Catholic Primary School, Stalybridge

LITTLE RED LOCKET AND THE DRAGON

Little Locket's mother said, 'Go and take these to
your cousin's house, your auntie is not very well.'
She wandered into the forest and went into a cave
that belonged to a dragon! After she had seen him he
breathed fire and gobbled up poor Little Red Locket.

ANDREW BETTS (9)
St Peter's Catholic Primary School, Stalybridge

THE TRIP TO EARTH

The spaceship was ready to take off to the most popular planet in space, Earth. Zitren started the engine and heard a loud *bang!* It took off as fast as lightning. In a blink of an eye, he was on Earth. Zitren was the first alien ever to visit Earth.

ELLIOT RYAN (10)

St Peter's Catholic Primary School, Stalybridge

THE CABBAGE OF THE CARRIAGE

The angel godmother waved her staff, 'Get this girl a
marvellous carriage to take her to the ball!'
Princess Rose, was blinded by the flash. When she
could see, there was a huge green cabbage.
'I said carriage, *not* cabbage!' the angel godmother
shrieked. 'I'll try again,' she said softly …

VICTORIA GREENHAIGH (10)
St Peter's Catholic Primary School, Stalybridge

HUMPTY

Humpty was a happy egg. He had lots of friends and
they all sat on a wall singing. But one rainy day eight
eggs fell off. Humpty was very sad and cried and
cried. Humpty was all alone.
The next day Humpty fell off and nobody saw
Humpty again.

AMY WALKER (10)

St Peter's Catholic Primary School, Stalybridge

TWINKLE BOND

Twinkle was upset about all the comets in space, they were killing her friends and family. Twinkle was out once and the comets were going to attack Bill, her best friend. She dived in front of Bill and got hit by the comets. Poor Twinkle was then in hospital.

ELIZABETH O'BRIEN (10)
St Peter's Catholic Primary School, Stalybridge

THE PIRATE SHIP

There was a pirate ship. It stayed in the same place.
One day a spy came along and was curious. He hired
a boat and went to the ship. Then he got on the ship
and the pirates caught him with rope. He had a knife
and got free.

ELLIE CROSBY (10)
St Peter's Catholic Primary School, Stalybridge

NO NAME THE ALIEN!

No Name was strolling down the street like every other normal day for him when some bullies came up to him and started pushing him around. No Name didn't like this. He asked them to stop. They said no so he ripped his skin off and scared them away.

OLIVER MARSHALL-WELCH (10)

St Peter's Catholic Primary School, Stalybridge

TARA BOND 007

There was an almighty screech as she sped around
the corner.
'You must hurry!' Jonathan's nearly there!' yelled 001.
'I'm on my way,' replied 007.
Yep, there was another emergency in New York,
but could 007 save Shannon her best friend from a
terrible fate? Only time will tell.

TARA MONAGHON-JOHN (10)
St Peter's Catholic Primary School, Stalybridge

THE GLASS MURDERER

Ping! It hit the floor. Coated in blood. One man lay
near. Fast as light. Who had the guts? Who was the
knife made of glass, the gun and the bullet too? Why?
Why?
Well only one person Mr Scarma, the glass murderer.
Come on, kill him, the glass murderer.

HARRISON GIBSON (11)

St Peter's Catholic Primary School, Stalybridge

WHITE TACKMAN VS BLUE TACKMAN

Once there was White Tackman and his evil friend, Blue Tackman. They wanted a war on the battlefield but White Tackman didn't turn up because he had no weapons. Once he came back the war began but one survived. Suddenly…

LUKE DERWENT (10)

St Peter's Catholic Primary School, Stalybridge

HUMPTY DUMPTY

Humpty Dumpty started to sing. *Crash! Bang! Wallop!*
Humpty Dumpty fell off the wall. Soldiers started
charging on horses towards him. They then tried to
put him together again. Sadly they couldn't put him
together so they galloped back to the kingdom.
Humpty Dumpty never sang again!

NIAMH MCGAHAN (10)
St Peter's Catholic Primary School, Stalybridge

COACH OF THE DEVIL

On New Year's Eve a rich man, Skene, ordered his coach driver to drive across the loch of Skene. Skene said he was not to look back.
Halfway across the driver couldn't resist and looked back. He saw Skene sitting next to the Devil. He was never seen again!

SAM BLEWITT (11)
St Peter's Catholic Primary School, Stalybridge

WORLD'S FINEST DAY

The day came, but only few knew about the world's final day. However, they all didn't believe it.
Ben, a young boy who did believe and knew what day it was, 15th December. He tried to warn everyone but they didn't listen. All hope was lost.

HENRY COCKER (10)
St Peter's Catholic Primary School, Stalybridge

DILL THE ELF

One day, there was a grumpy elf called Dill. He never spoke to the other elves, who wanted to be Dill's friend. A spirit came to Dill and showed him his past. The next day he spoke to all the elves and invited them over. Dill never ever sinned again.

BETHANY LEWIS (11)
St Peter's Catholic Primary School, Stalybridge

DEEP BLUE SEA

One day three men went on a fishing trip. Suddenly a large object struck the boat with immense power. It knocked one man overboard. The water was now cloudy and the man was dragged under by an octopus! The water turned red and they never saw their friend again.

LUCAS SWEENEY (10)
St Peter's Catholic Primary School, Stalybridge

UNTITLED

Lizzie got home. There was a note that read, *Me and your dad - gone for tea.*
Lizzie went in - the tap was running in the bathroom, she was scared. She went in, it was her gran in the bath.
'Hi Lizzie, didn't your mum tell you I was here?'

MILLY LUBY (10)

St Peter's Catholic Primary School, Stalybridge

THE NATIVITY (RETOLD)

Sheila and Richard travelled to Manchester after Nurse Debra told them that Sheila would give birth to baby Peter who would be an eco warrior. All that was left to sleep in was the Premier Inn. Peter was born. Waiters and MPs came and bared their gifts.

SARAH DRISCOLL (11)
Sacred Heart Catholic Primary School

THE THREE BEARS AND GOLDILOCKS

Goldilocks was tired after her long walk. She was ready to put her feet up and rest. Entering the house three bowls caught her eye. 'How did they get there?' Confused she went upstairs for a rest, tripping over a chair leg! Upstairs in her bed were three sleeping bears!

DANIEL WHITE (11)

Sacred Heart Catholic Primary School

CHRISTMAS PRESENTS

I was told I couldn't have anymore Christmas
presents because my parents spent the money
in Conwy and bought me a digital camera. I was
devastated but I understood. Then I
saw loads of bags in the shed. I took a peek.
Think I'll have a white Christmas after all!

ANGELICA FULGENCIO (10)

Sacred Heart Catholic Primary School

FRIENDS FOREVER!

I was really hoping that one day, in the future, she would come and visit me. If she didn't come I would go looking for her when I was older. Whatever happens we will always be best friends forever! I can tell.

CHARLOTTE CLARKE (11)

Sacred Heart Catholic Primary School

SURPRISE!

Ella was in her front room all alone because her
mother and father had nipped out. Even though she
was a big girl she was scared. 'Oh no, Mum and Dad
aren't back and it's Christmas Eve.'
Ella waited until nine o'clock.
Suddenly, 'Surprise!'
What a great surprise party.

REBECCA MALONEY (10)
Sacred Heart Catholic Primary School

THE BULLY

Katie walked slowly into the school field with her heart beating against her chest.

'Oh no,' said Katie, 'here comes Becky Taler, the bully.'

'Hey you, come here,' said Becky who gave Katie a really hard thud in the belly.

Mrs Lane saw Becky and sent her to detention.

RACHEL HOUGH (11)
Sacred Heart Catholic Primary School

ALEX THE ACROBAT

Alex was talented, he could do so many things. He was a clown, an acrobat, a juggler, a bareback rider and even a flea trainer. But how could he use his talents? One day a circus came to his town. Could this be the answers to all of his problems?

LAUREN NEVILLE (10)

Sacred Heart Catholic Primary School

CHARLIE AND THE CHOCOLATE FACTORY

Charlie was the last one, the other four children had gone, flushed away, blown up, dumped and miniaturised. Willy Wonka, the owner of the factory, smiled, 'You have done it, Charlie, the factory is yours. But I will be the Assistant Manager!'

KIERAN ARMSTRONG (11)

Sacred Heart Catholic Primary School

JACK AND JILL

Jack and Jill went up a mountain to fetch a pile of sweets, when Jack came down he had a frown since Jill ate all the sweets. Then Jill was sick and Jack was happy.

BRIAN ALLDRED (11)

Sacred Heart Catholic Primary School

THE THREE ROBBER PIGS

The three pigs got in a straw house and stole a DVD player. They went to a stick house and stole a television. They went to a brick house but when they went in there was a wolf policeman waiting for them.
'I've got you now boys!'

KEIRAN CRIPPS (10)

Sacred Heart Catholic Primary School

SURPRISE PARTY

Jay walked into the dark house. Nobody was there.
Suddenly he heard a noise. His family jumped out
'Surprise!'
'Argh!' Jay was shocked, he ran out frightened.
Why would they jump out at him … and then he
remembered.

ETHAN RAZAK (11)

Sacred Heart Catholic Primary School

SURPRISE PARTY

Mr Walker ran to his house, there was a dog chasing
him. He jumped to his door, opened it and …
'Surprise!'
'What a great surprise,' Mr Walker said.

SEBASTIAN RAV KINTANA NAUNGAYAN (10)

Sacred Heart Catholic Primary School

MATILDA'S MAGIC MOMENT

'Open,' Matilda pointed at the curtains. She was astonished, they opened! Matilda started to point at everything. Cards were flying everywhere, music playing, drawers, cupboards opening and shutting. Matilda was enjoying every moment. She was dancing her socks off. Matilda jumped and jumped and jumped for joy! Then it stopped.

BETHANY ATTWOOD (10)
Sacred Heart Catholic Primary School

THE ENORMOUS CARROT

Once a farmer planted some seeds, one grew and
grew! He said to his wife, 'We'll have that for tea.'
He pulled with all his might, nothing.
The boy across the lane shouted, 'Want some help?'
Farmer said, 'Please.'
Nothing.
Everybody came to help, eventually it came out!

DOMINIC O'BRIEN (10)
Sacred Heart Catholic Primary School

THE STONE

Joe went to the beach to collect stones. He found a cave, it was pitch-black. He slowly walked into the cave, he saw a golden flash. Joe went further down; he could see a glittering gold stone!

JORDON SAMPSON (10)

Sacred Heart Catholic Primary School

HAPPY ENDING

One day there was a boy who lived in his house with his father. They were very poor. This boy did not have a mother. One day a wizard came to help the boy and his father and the boy got a very kind mother. They lived happily ever after.

JAKE GIBSON (7)
The Firs School

BEST FRIENDS

Dennis and James were playing hide-and-seek.
James couldn't find Dennis at all. He looked in lots of
places and Dennis was not there. Suddenly he saw
something move in a tree. James spied Dennis behind
some leaves.
'Hurrah!' cheered James. Then they went for a drink
and biscuits.

JAMES HARRIS (8)

The Firs School

THE QUARRY

'Hey, let's go to the quarry Nathan,' Tom said. So that's what they did. They climbed up and down and played loads of games. Oh how much fun it was! Then they played hide-and-seek, but Tom couldn't find Nathan. He looked and looked then …
'Boo!' Nathan jumped out.

BARNABY JONES (7)

The Firs School

CHRISTMAS NIGHT

It was a dark and scary night and I woke up. I went down the stairs. Halfway I heard some footsteps. I ran back to my bed.
It was Santa Claus walking in the sitting room. It sounded like he had a very big bag of toys for us.

MAX WILD (7)

The Firs School

A DREAM

One windy night a strange noise woke Lucy. She got up and looked under her bed. Her toy box lid was opening and closing. She found a hole in the bottom of the box and a ladder going down. She climbed to the bottom and saw dinosaurs running towards her!

CLAUDIA MINCHIN (7)
The Firs School

HOME ALONE

Ben ran upstairs to find his favourite toy. He came down; his family had driven off down the road. Oh no, he was home alone.

Two men appeared, sneaking around. Ben set a trap so they could not get in.

His mum returned delighted Ben had beaten the robbers.

JACK BODEN (7)

The Firs School

THE BIG BAD FOX

Once upon a time the fox blew down the granny's
house. The fox ate Goldilocks and the fox trapped
one piggy and chased another piggy. He went down
the other chimney and burnt his bottom and they
lived happily ever after in their own house.

SAM BERGIN (7)
The Firs School

SCARY STORY

Once upon a time there was a man who was called Freddy, he was a woodcutter. He saw a tree, a magic tree. The tree was looking at him. The magic tree said, 'Come here.' He did. Then the tree said, 'Happy Hallowe'en.' The man went.

ZAIN SHAHZAD (8)

The Firs School

THE DRAGON MYSTERY

There was once a dragon who was good but he pushed people into rivers. The people did not care. Once a day came when the dragon's mum died, his mum was very special to him. The dragon was very upset so the dragon decided to stop pushing people into rivers.

NATASHA KIMBER (7)

The Firs School

111

THE OLD HOUSE

James lived across the street from an old house. One
day he walked over to the house. The door was
open so he walked inside. He heard a strange noise
and ran into the house. As he ran he fell through the
floor. What happened to James? No one knows.

CHARLES MAYOR (7)

The Firs School

THE BEAST

Once upon a time there lived a beast; he was friendly but lonely because everyone was afraid of him. The beast was thirsty, he went to find a river but he fell in and sank. Luckily a mermaid saved him. They ate fish and chips and fell in everlasting love.

AMELIA DIGGLE (7)
The Firs School

113

FLAT MAN

Once there was a boy that was flat, his name was Rob. He was ten years old; he had no friends because he was flat. One day a new boy came to Rob's school, his name was Zain. He said, 'Can I be your friend?'
Rob said, 'Yes!'

JAMES CLINTON-HUNT (7)

The Firs School

THE MUD MONSTER

I entered the dark creepy woods in search of
firewood. In the distance I observed something
moving in the brown murky swamp. I walked
cautiously towards the dark terrifying waters. Up
jumped a springy brown monster, it was Matty!
'Playing in the mud again?' I asked.
'Yes,' confessed Matty.

HARRI DICKINSON (9)
The Marlborough Primary School

APOLLO 13

'We have lift-off!'
Apollo 13 was on the moon. After a while exploring they headed back to the shuttle only to find a huge hole. A rumbling sound commenced and a Martian jumped out and said, in his alien language, 'Eeeeee.' The astronauts were stranded for life!

ALEX HOLT (9)

The Marlborough Primary School

TEATIME

One hot sunny day a little girl left her cottage and walked down to the pond. She got out her fishing rod and quickly caught a fish. She ran back home and her mum said, 'Wow, what a clever girl you are, let's cook it for our delicious evening meal.'

AMY TURNOCK (9)
The Marlborough Primary School

117

THE EVIL ROBOT

'Wow, this is the best present in the world,' gasped
Jim. 'It does anything you say.'
Firstly he made it do all his homework.
Unfortunately his brother snatched the robot from
Jim and yelled, 'Take over the world!'
Subsequently, the robot did just as Jim's brother
asked.

ADAM SMITH (9)
The Marlborough Primary School

THE MYSTERY FACE OF CHRISTMAS

The night sky was out as a mystery face walked by.
The mystery face jumped down people's chimneys
saying, 'Ho, ho, ho!' The person went down my
chimney so I ran downstairs, I found Santa dancing to
my favourite CD.
'Surprise,' he said happily, 'Merry Christmas to all'

LAURA WHISTON (9)
The Marlborough Primary School

KILLER HILL

The mist was rolling in, and the runners could just be seen as they ran the dreaded course through mud and rain. Katie was lagging behind at the back. She struggled to keep with the others as they entered Killer Hill. The pain was immense, would it beat her?

SARAH WHEELTON (9)
The Marlborough Primary School

TO DREAM OR NOT TO DREAM

Eleanor came home at midnight - the spookiest time. As she turned the platinum key it seemed as if the gargoyles turned to look at her. She crept up the stairs hoping to make no noise but the squeaky floorboards wouldn't be quiet … then *bang!* It was just a disturbing dream.

ELEANOR SMITH (10)
The Marlborough Primary School

THE GIRL AND THE FISH

One day a girl went for a walk, she found a pond so she got her fishing rod out. The girl kept on trying to catch the fish and she finally did.
After a while she went home with the fish and her mum had it for tea.

NATASHA HEATH (10)
The Marlborough Primary School

AN ALIEN ENCOUNTER

John went to a warehouse. On the way he thought
he saw a UFO. He did! He ran to the nearest
telephone box and tried to make contact with the
aliens. He did! He thought they said, 'Trick or treat?'
He'd forgotten it was Hallowe'en.

FORBES HUNTER (9)
The Marlborough Primary School

THE MONSTER SCARE

Long ago, in a scary place called Dagibz, there was a very remote place. No one ever went in and came out alive. Once a boy went in, he was not scared of anything until he came to a halt. A big, scary, petrifying, killing monster! He got eaten instantly.

BILLY SCHOFIELD (9)
The Marlborough Primary School

THREE LITTLE KITTENS

Three little kittens started to play but it got a bit out of hand. They leapt off the sofa and crashed into the television. Then, after running into the kitchen, they climbed into the fridge. They ate some pudding then shot up to the bedroom and pounced on the pillow.

LAURA NANCOLLIS (10)
The Marlborough Primary School

THE NASTY DOG

One night a girl went to bed. In the middle of the night she heard a noise. She looked out of the window and saw a dog. It broke into the house. The girl shut her door; the dog broke in her bedroom. The dog attacked the girl ...

NATHAN EDWARDS (9)
The Marlborough Primary School

SANTA SAGA

It was a dark silent night and there was a faint jingle of bells. Suddenly, there was a thud on the icy roof! Firstly a 'Ho, ho, … whee.' *Plop!* Santa got stuck in the chimney. Then there was an 'Ooh, ooh.' Santa's bum was burning!
'More mince pies for me!'

MEGAN STEPHENS (9)
The Marlborough Primary School

THE BOY WHO CRIED WOLF

Once there was a boy who always lied. He went to bed and heard a noise every night. One night he got out of bed and went into the garden. He walked until he saw it was a wolf. The boy screamed and he shouted, 'Wolf!'

No one came.

JAMES BETHELL (10)

The Marlborough Primary School

SCREAM!

It was a dark stormy night. I was in a cold misty graveyard; I was alone, very alone. Suddenly the trees rustled as if someone was there. I convinced myself I was safe but I was wrong. Just then I felt a bony hand close around my neck. Then, silence ...

SERENA BELL-LU (10)
The Marlborough Primary School

TRIANGLE OF DEATH

One day a pirate ship got lost in the graveyard for
ships, never to be seen again.
Two hundred years later, a cruise ship went for a
tour of the graveyard. The cruise ship collided with
the lost pirate ship. It was so badly damaged it sank,
it was lost forever.

THOMAS J CREWE (9)
The Marlborough Primary School

THE ADVENTURE OF CAPTAIN UNDERPANTS

In the land of Sock, Harold and George were friends with Captain Underpants. The land came under invasion by the Terrortime Toilets. They tried to take over Sockland by stealing everyone's socks. Captain Underpants, Harold and George battled the Terrortime Toilets and won back the socks. Sockland was saved.

CALLUM ALLMAN (10)
The Marlborough Primary School

THE NEW DOG

There was once a little girl who wanted a dog badly.
She begged her mum and dad, they refused but
reminded her her birthday was soon.
The day of her birthday finally came and she woke up
excitedly. She ran downstairs, opened her presents
and there was a dog!

LIBBY BULL (10)
The Marlborough Primary School

RUN AWAY TED

Jane had a teddy bear called Ted. The problem with
Ted was he kept running away. Every night Jane
would find him missing whilst Ted would run over the
fields trying to escape. Then one day Jane's mum told
her to put butter on his feet which stopped him!

OLIVER SIMKISS (9)
The Marlborough Primary School

133

YOU CAN BE SAFE

It was a cold and windy night, Sammy was jogging
home. He had to go through a forest. The forest was
dark and cold. The poor boy was frightened, then he
heard a noise. There was an old man.
'Stop!' said the man. So he did and then went home.

PHOEBE MCCARTHY (9)
The Marlborough Primary School

THE STORY OF SANTA

It was time. He was all set to go. The sleigh lifted up
as Santa left his workshop on Christmas Eve.
'Ho, ho, ho! Merry Christmas,' chanted Santa.
By then Santa was in the sky and had by now
delivered nine thousand presents, he was in France
... then he crashed!

REBECCA QUINN (9)
The Marlborough Primary School

THE LONELY HOUSE

The dark wooden door creaked as I stepped into the lonely house. The walls were lit with dancing candles. Inside, the stairs led up to a room - a dark room. As I walked into the room the door slammed behind me. I felt a cold bony hand on my shoulder ...

OLIVIA HUDSON (11)
The Marlborough Primary School

SUSAN'S SEARCH FOR SANTA

It was Christmas Eve. People were charging around
to get their last minute presents. Susan went over to
see Santa. When she got there Santa was gone.
No Santa, no Christmas! She searched high and low.
She still couldn't find him. She walked around the
corner, there he was ...
'Santa!'

NICOLA HODGKISS (11)
The Marlborough Primary School

KINDER AND THE CLONE

Kinder made a clone of himself. It copied everything that Kinder did. Kinder got tired of the clone and went to switch him off. But the clone walked away. So, Kinder scratched his back and when clone Kinder scratched too it hit its off button. Kinder celebrated as he'd won!

GEORGE WILLIAMS (10)

The Marlborough Primary School

THE DEFEAT

There it was, stood in front of me, the most horrific monster ever. It had teeth like knives and claws like daggers. The monster drew a sharp sword. He wanted a fight. I gulped and backed up, bending down. I threw a stick at the monster. Was the monster dead?

JESSICA SIMMS (10)
The Marlborough Primary School

THE LAMBORGHINI

I was walking down the street when I saw a
Lamborghini. It had a huge boot and a large engine.
It was so shiny, I could see my reflection in the
window! I would win all the girls; take them for rides
all day!
Oops, it just got towed away!

JAMES KITE (10)
The Marlborough Primary School

LOWEST INSTITUTE VILLAINOUS EDUCATION

'Welcome to LIVE, the villainous school!' greeted the red hologram.

'What the ...?' murmured Spike, 'I don't want to be a villain.'

Then ... *ting!* Spike had a plan.

After ten seconds the hologram showed them to the dinner hall. Spike could smell explosives. Spike slammed the button, *boom!*

'Bye-bye school!'

CHARLOTTE SMITH (10)
The Marlborough Primary School

MY CHOCOLATE CAKE

There was a chocolate cake. It was nice with some sprinkles and mouth-watering - a cake that you could not resist. It was sponge cake with jam in the middle of it. It had some icing. Then my sister came in and took it.

'I will have this,' she shouted.

MICHAEL LYON (10)

The Marlborough Primary School

THE CHOCOLATE BAR

There was a chocolate bar. It was so yummy, all the girls wanted it. It was delicious, I bought it. I was the envy of my friends. It had a milk chocolate topping, a wafer-thin middle. It was mouth-watering. I walked down the road, tripped, it went *mush!*

JAMIE DOOK (10)
The Marlborough Primary School

THE MILLION POUND NOTE

I was walking down the street when I saw something.
It was a million pound note!
'I'm rich! I can get a Ferrari, a mansion. Everything
I've always wanted.'
I was so busy shouting I didn't even pick it up. The
wind blew. The note fell in the gutter!

CONOR DAY (11)
The Marlborough Primary School

FRUSTRATION

I was driving down the road when I saw a PlayStation
3 for £200! I rushed in, I rushed to the counter.
Then there was a big fuss about it. I was too busy
daydreaming that someone else bought it! I was
furious and shouted, 'Who bought it? *Nooo!*'

TOM PROFFITT (11)
The Marlborough Primary School

UNTITLED

It was Christmas Eve. I was staring at the roasted peanuts. Mum called me for bed, up I went. I had to have them so after Mum and Dad went to bed I sneaked for them. I scoffed all of them but when I went upstairs, Mum was there, busted!

LUCY HEYWOOD (10)

The Marlborough Primary School

WET MONKEY

I could see, it looked so marvellous, it was a gun! I grabbed hold of it and aimed it at a monkey called Fluffo. I pulled the trigger and missed. It hit a tree which fell over so I shot again and hit the monkey. It was a water pistol.

JACK LOCKETT (10)
The Marlborough Primary School

THE HOLE OF HORROR

One day I was walking down a dark street and I saw a big house. It was abandoned! The door was covered with cobwebs and the windows were smeared with dust. I started to walk towards the house and tripped in a hole. Unfortunately that was the end of me!

KIMBERLEY WELBOURN (11)

The Marlborough Primary School

ALIEN INVADER

One day me and my brother went to buy a brand
new game called Alien Invader, it cost thirty-nine
pounds. My mum wouldn't lend us the money but we
really needed the game. We stole the money from
my mean mum. Wickedly we bought it and played!

THOMAS MARKEY (10)
The Marlborough Primary School

149

THE FIRST WAY TO OPEN A COCONUT

Scribble and Scramble were swinging in the trees when Scribble found something shiny on the ground. He climbed down and picked it up. It was a new one pound coin. He didn't know that! He carried on while Scramble found a coconut and hit Scribble on the head.

'Yum … milk!'

MATTHEW BELL (10)

The Marlborough Primary School

BEST FRIEND

There lived a boy called Fred. He went to his mate's house and his mum said he had to walk. He did. On his way he saw a castle. It was haunted. Fred went in and there was a ghost but the ghost wanted Fred as his best friend.

ISSIE JENNINGS (10)
The Marlborough Primary School

151

CUP FINAL

It's cup Final day. Reece Rovers vs Markey Hotspurs,
the match begins. John blasts the ball in the net.
1-0 Rovers! Bobby Bruiser bombs the bouncing ball
against Tommy Tucker's bum! It goes in.
The final whistle blows, 2-0 to Reece Rovers. Reece
Rovers wins the Year Cup!

REECE MASSEY (10)
The Marlborough Primary School

THE BUG

I was dragging my feet to school. There was this egg
that was made of metal. I picked it up and twisted it
open, a bug fell out! I started thinking it was nothing I
had ever seen.

'I'll be rich!'

But it scuttled away and got stood on.

'Doh!'

EDWARD TAYLOR-BROWN (10)

The Marlborough Primary School

ISSIE AND THE EVIL DOLL

There once lived a little girl called Issie. She loved
dolls. One day a special dolly arrived at her house.
From the minute she opened it she played all day
with it.
At night it awoke, grabbed a knife, looked at the
bedrooms and went in to kill!

MADDY CONNELLY (11)
The Marlborough Primary School

STRANGERS

The red-haired boy had lived at number 73 for five years now. Despite that, Jack had only ever seen him twice. Thinking about it, Jack hadn't seen anyone going in or out of that house. There were heavy curtains at the windows but you knew he was there, watching ...

JACK SANDERS (10)
The Meadows Primary School

SARAH

Sitting by a warm burning fire Sarah gulped down a roasting cup of cocoa with marshmallows, a Flake and cream on top. Eventually she drifted off into an effortless dreamy sleep.

Awaking in the morning she found the fire crackling away and a beautiful bird chirping merrily at the window.

REBECCA LOUISE BOULT (10)

The Meadows Primary School

THE NEW WORLD

One night a boy named Daniel discovered a new world of adventure. He didn't tell anyone, not even his family.

Every night, at midnight, he ran into his new world. One day he stepped in and everything had changed completely. It turned into a battlefield of war. It was destroyed!

DANIEL FOX (10)

The Meadows Primary School

THE MONSTER

It was twelve o'clock, Joe couldn't get to sleep. He was just about to nod off when he heard a groan and a scream. He thought, *is it a monster?* He stepped carefully out of bed and opened the door. He saw his brother standing there in his pyjamas!

JOE MINSHALL (10)
The Meadows Primary School

BIG VS LITTLE

Feeling helpless I pulled, it felt like forever. Suddenly the big figure (who was also trying to get the rope) let go and I went tumbling over the emerald-green grass. Shaking my night-black, hairy coat I wagged my tail with delight. I'd won!

JAKE MAGEE (10)
The Meadows Primary School

BYE-BYE MONEY

Blustering wind lifted sand from the beach, into swirling gusts like tornados. The sea crashed against my sandcastle and demolished it. Feeling unhappy, Mum asked if I'd like an ice cream. Giving me a five pound note I set off with a smile but the wind was too strong!

'Oops!'

LOGAN WESTWICK (9)

The Meadows Primary School

PONY HORROR

This morning I met up with my friends, Olivia and Lucy. We went riding on our ponies but they were excited and bolted off. The ponies were spooked and we all fell off! There was something coming towards us. They all had knives. What should we do?

KATIE SMITH (11)
The Meadows Primary School

THE LOST RABBIT

'Where's Fluffy?' cried Jack.
'I don't know,' shouted Bob.
'Do you think he escaped last night when the repair
man came?' Jack said sadly.
'He could have,' Bob shouted.
They looked around the village and couldn't find
Fluffy so they went home.
'I wonder if he is in the garage.'

JACK CHALLINOR (9)

The Meadows Primary School

INFORMATION

We hope you have enjoyed reading this book - and that you will continue to enjoy it in the coming years.

If you like reading and writing, drop us a line or give us a call and we'll send you a free information pack. Alternatively visit our website at www.youngwriters.co.uk

Write to:
Young Writers Information,
Remus House,
Coltsfoot Drive,
Peterborough,
PE2 9JX

Tel: (01733) 890066
Email: youngwriters@forwardpress.co.uk